MOUNTAIN MURDERS

MOUNTAIN MURDERS

Joyce Zeck

CHAPTER ONE

MY NAME IS Julie and my sister in law is Sue and we were working in my flower beds in my front yard on a hot Thursday in May. Sue has been my sister in law for 19 years and we have the same taste in flowers. We were close to quitting when an ordinary blue Chevy panel van slowed and pulled to a stop on the side of the road in my yard. The gentleman who got out of the van looked like any middle aged farmer, coveralls and all. Once we approached him we saw he was a very ugly man. His deformed face was mean looking. He said he was looking for a place that was for sale in the area and was lost he was holding a map. Sue and I approached to see if we could help, that's when he pulled out a pistol hidden by the map and said, get in the back of the van. We had no choice I don't care what anyone says when a gun is pointed at you; you do what you are told. Once in the van we realized it was a large padded metal box, no way we could escape or be heard yelling. We where both dressed for working in the yard, t-tops and shorts, no place for cell phones, because they would have fallen out when we when bent over. We fell to the floor as he took off down the road; he drove for hours and would not stop for anything. We finally fell asleep lying on the vans cold padded floor and woke when he stopped to open a gate and back into his yard.

When he opened the door it was fading evening light, but brighter than the interior of the van. He told us this would be our home for the rest of our lives. He told us to take off all our cloths and put them in the back of the van. At first we hesitated, but once he shoved the gun in our faces we did as told. I had once in my younger days, I am 62 years old and Sue if 51 years old, been in a nudist colony so taking off my cloths did not bother me as much as it did Sue, she stood there crying. He slapped her and told her to stop or she would get more of the pain.

He then showed us the fact that the place was surrounded by a white board fence topped with barbwire as far as you could see and from there chain link fence topped with barbwire and this was why we were not allowed to have cloths that could help in escaping. He stated he had 100 hundred acres and all of it was surrounded in this way. The fence is on a concrete foundation one foot in the ground so digging out was not an option since most of his land was on a mountain top full of rock.

He proceeded to take us to what he called the bunkhouse where the other women where. He said there were three other women there and they would fill us in on what was going to been happening to us. He told an older black woman named Bertha to take care of us which she did. Bertha showed us around.

The bunkhouse was one large room, where the commode and shower was exposed to the rest of the room. There were 10 cots even though he never had more than five women there at a time. There was an old fashion black wood burning cook stove and a dining table and six chairs.

CHAPTER TWO

B ERTHA TOLD US a story that chilled us to the bone, while she showed us the bathroom and fed us.

Bertha was a light skinned black woman 47 years old and was the first woman he caught and brought to his farm. She was a good cook, but not much help in his two gardens. The first garden was for food and the second was for his pot (marijuana). So he took more women as needed. They as well as the two of us would work in the gardens, eat and sleep naked in the bunkhouse. The only other thing he wanted from his women was for his sexual needs, when, where and whatever he wanted. His sexual needs were based on how much pain he could inflict.

Bertha pretty much stayed to herself, she had been there 20 years and was now 47 years old but acted 70.

The rest of the story came from Betty, Sally and Brenda.

Two of the women were white, Betty short 5'0" and stocky about 35 years old had been there about 10 years and Brenda tall and lanky 6'0" who was 46 and had been there 12 years. Sally was a young 23 year old dark black woman about 5'6" and muscular who had been there about 5 years.

Betty kept to herself because she could not take in all that had happened to her, she did what she was told and that was all.

Brenda and Sally would talk to us but only at night when the lights were out, because he was known to spy on them to see if they were trying to break out. If he thought they were planning *anything* he would beat them with a belt the next morning and make them work with their backs bleeding in the hot sun. Once was enough of that for anyone.

We were too tired to talk much that first night, knowing what we had in store for us in the morning.

CHAPTER THREE

T HE NEXT MORNING we were awakened at first light, given time to wash and eat then to the fields. We would stop by the tool shed and were given whatever tools we needed for the day. Our first day was hoeing the vegetable garden, which was about two acres. The morning was not too bad and when we stopped for lunch we only began to feel the heat, but by day's end we were blistered from sun and wind and could hardy move. Both Sue and I had a tan from working in our yards but were not prepared for this.

We were told not to complain because he would beat us on top of the sunburn. There was no medicine for anyone and the others were not allowed to help us in anyway. The only thing we could do was stand in a cold shower and relieve some of the heat. If we could not make it we would be taken to a 50 foot ravine and thrown in to die a very long and horrible death. Of course we did not get much sleep that night either.

Being the oldest and heaviest there it made a lot of things harder for me than the others. But I would not complain and seem like a baby to the others. I wanted to keep up my end of this hell.

The next morning we thought we would go back to the vegetable garden, but no we went to the pot garden and it was in shade most of the day. Don't think for a minute that it was any easier to work with a much blistered back, but at least the shade did not make it any worse. By the day's end of hoeing and carrying water to the plants it was all we could do to eat and shower.

Brenda asked Bertha for some tampons. Brenda said she would not have to work the next day. We asked why she didn't have to work. Brenda said in the beginning when Bertha had her first period there he did not know about that. Bertha sent him to the store to get tampons and said tell them that your 13 year old daughter just started her period and you needed them for her. But he had no idea what they were or where to look for them. The lady in the pharmacy a grandmotherly type showed him and said she thought she would need the large size and the pack of 36.

She said if she did not use all of them this time she could use the rest next month. He asked how often this happened and she looked at him funny and said once a month for about a week. That the first day she should stay in bed so as not to bleed too much, but after that she could do whatever she wanted. She then asked where his wife was and he said he wished he knew. This made the woman feel better about this strange man and his request.

CHAPTER FOUR

THE NEXT DAY brought the hardest pain of all, I had to stand by and watch as he raped Sue. He took her right there in the vegetable garden on her very sore back in front of Sally and me. Sally signaled not to do anything it would make things worse. He made Sue go back to work when he was finished with her. He made it clear that I would be next, but I would not know when or where.

He came that night to my bed and hurt me as much as he could think to do. The others had to pretend to be asleep and not listen to my screams, for scream I did loud and clear. Crying came after he left I would not give he the pleasure of seeing me cry.

The next morning I could not move, getting out of bed was beyond the question. When I did not come out to get my tools for the day he came looking for me, mad as hell. I told him if he wanted to throw me away go ahead or he could wait one day and I would be back to work. Did he really want to go looking for someone else so soon? He thought about it for a while then said no he would give me one day and if I could not go back to work then he would throw me in the ravine. I did something then I should not have and that was I asked a question.

The question was had he thought of putting his life in a book, of course it could not be published while he lived, but it could be added to year after year and he would have it to read over as he got older. He laughed at me and stated I was crazier than he was.

I went back to work the next day and the next and the next. Life for us women was the same old same old every day, except for when he wanted sex. Those days or nights got to be the only thing to look forward to, only because it was different. We got to making bets on who would be next.

After a couple of weeks of this Sue began to be like Betty not talking and upset all the time. Sally and Brenda and I played cards and other games but we also talked after dark.

Sally had a husband and two children, a boy and a girl that kept her going.

Brenda had just her family, mom and dad, three sisters and two brothers. She wanted to see her parents one more time before they passed away, they both were in there 80's now. Just when it seemed there was nothing out of the ordinary going to happen he came to me and said he wanted me to write his book.

CHAPTER FIVE

H E SAID I was smarter than any of the others he had found over the years and he thought he could trust me to write the true story. We set in the kitchen of the house the only room he would allow me in. The wooden kitchen table looked as if he had been there since the house had been built. He had gone to the store and bought paper and pencils for me to work with. Here is what he told me over the next couple of weeks:

He name was Mike Harden, 54 years old, and he was born in Ohio (where in Ohio he would not say). His father beat him all the time for no reason other than his ugly face. His mother sexually abused him from the time he could remember around age four and probably younger. Life growing up on a pig and cow farm was no fun and being the only child left them no one else to abuse but him. When he was sixteen he ran away from home and went to work on the railroad doing whatever he could find to do.

Note: that I will never refer to him in this book by anything other than he, his or him, I hate this man and will not say his name again.

One day he was cleaning out the box cars when he found a satchel full of money. When he got to his room he counted it and found $356,000 dollars in the bag. He was set for life, but he was not going to stay in Ohio. He decided to go south instead of west. He ended up in a bar in West Virginia and won the 100 acres he now lives on.

He had no skills so he paid to have the house built and later when he decided to find a woman the fence was installed. He knew somehow deep inside that with his ugly looks, his sexual needs and need for pot that no woman in her right mind would marry him. So after about 5 years of no woman he decided to kidnap one, which led to another and another a total of 25 over the next 20 years.

I got him to tell me about each woman as he picked them up and their stories follow in the next chapters.

CHAPTER SIX

H E DECIDED TO go to a small town in the middle of nowhere to hunt for his first woman. He parked in a super market parking lot and leaned on the side of his van with a map out. When a woman came out that was parked close he would asked them if they could help him. What the woman saw was a white ugly farmer with his map out and they felt he was safe enough to speak too. When the one he wanted came along he pointed the gun hidden in the map at them.

His first victim was a light skinned black woman named Bertha, no last name per her request.

Bertha was a young mother of 25 with three boys and stubborn as anyone, but seeing that gun she climbed into the van. He took her purse and made sure she had no cell phone. There was no seat so she set on the floor and after a couple of hours fell asleep. She woke when he stopped the van to open the gate and back in the yard. He told her to undress and put her cloths in the van including her shoes. She said she was a Christian woman and he could go to hell because she would not do it.

He hit her hard enough to knock her down and she did as she was told.

He then told the speech that he would tell all the others for the next 20 years: This would be her home for the rest of her life, that his 100 acres was surrounded by a fence 10 feet tall and topped with barbwire and buried on top of a foot of concrete. No clothes meant no way to climb over and one foot of concrete meant no digging to get out.

He took Bertha to what he called the bunkhouse told her she would be the cook and work in his gardens during the day. It was very late when they arrived so the first thing he wanted was for her to cook super. She set down and refused to do anything forgetting already the bruise on her face. He grabbed her by her hair and dragged her to the stove. He placed her face next to the stove and asked her what she was going to do. Bertha said nothing; she did not believe he would hurt her. He said ok and pushed her face against the hot stove. When she yelled she do anything he wanted he pulled her away, leaving a burn over her right cheek, which would leave a very ugly scar, one she carries today. He had no heart and told her there was no medicine for her wounds and to fix supper now.

Bertha found all the necessary items needed to fix a steak dinner for both of them; even though she was not sure she should fix anything for herself because she did not feel like eating anything. When he came back to eat half an hour later he told her to eat with him. To keep him from getting mad at her again she ate a little. He explained while they ate that the next day she would get up at first light and fix breakfast for both of them. After breakfast she would go to the tool shed and get a hoe and work in the vegetable garden which was then only a half acre. She would stop and fix lunch for them and then return to the garden until done or he told her to stop to fix supper.

The next morning she did as told and had breakfast ready for him. When it was lunch time she was already sunburned, but he had no mercy for her and told her to fix lunch and then return to the garden. She was in so much pain from her face and back that she did very little hoeing. He came up from the pot garden about an hour before dark and she was not done. This made him mad and he went and knocked her down and screwed her right there. Her back was sunburned, but she would not cry out and give him the satisfaction of knowing she was in so much pain. Once he was finished he told her to get cleaned up and fix dinner right away. She stood in the shower as long as she could take it and then set and cried hoping he would not hear her. Her pride was deep and had cost her a lot already.

This was the way it would go for the next year cooking, working, and worrying about her kids and husband. Most of all waiting to find out when he would hurt her again which could be anytime, anywhere and anyway he wanted that would make her cry. He knew now to wait until she thought she was alone and he could hear her in the bunkhouse crying and laugh quietly to himself while he masturbated.

He finally got tired of her and wanted someone else; she was too slow in the garden. So he told her he was going hunting again for number two and that she would always be the cook and clean the bunkhouse and that was all, except for sex every now and then. Bertha could live with that.

CHAPTER SEVEN

HIS SECOND VICTIM was a young 17 year old, white tennis player named Kelly. Kelly is about 5'3" tall and very pretty.

He used the same operation this time as last hanging out in a super market parking lot. When Kelly got through tennis practice at her school, she worked in a pizza joint as a waitress. She pulled up beside his van and he asked her if she knew where a house on Strange Street was, it was supposed to be for sale and he was lost.

Kelly began to tell him that she did not know when he pulled his gun. She almost fainted. She pulled herself together and got in the van, hoping he would not take her cell phone, but of course he did.

The ride from this small town in the middle of nowhere took about four hours to make and Kelly cried herself to sleep. When she woke up he was shaking her awake and welcoming her to her new home. He told her to take off her clothes she refused and he slapped her so hard she passed out. He had Bertha to come help get her into the bunkhouse and throw her on a cot. Where she laid until Bertha woke her for super.

He came to super and could not keep from smiling and leering at Kelly.

All she wanted to do was curl up into a ball as tight as she could get. She did not want to eat and he told her to eat, did she think his food was not good enough for her little rich white ass? He said eat now or no food for breakfast, lunch and dinner tomorrow. Kelly did not believe him and did not eat. She took her shower and went to bed early because Bertha only told her the rules and wanted nothing else to do with her. Kelly felt like her world was coming to an end, she knew she could not do all the things Bertha told her she would have to.

The next morning he came and got her, even though he had to drag her to the tool shed. There he gave her a hoe and told her to follow him to the pot garden. She asked what he did with all the food and pot he grew. He told her the food is what they lived on, what they did not eat was sold at the farmer markets. The pot was also sold for the money to live on.

When it was time for Kelly to hoe she refused and he took off his belt and beat her until she said she would do what he wanted. The sun was not so bad in the pot garden and she already had a tan from playing tennis. Playing tennis and being in shape would help her survive as long as she did. But by lunch time she was ready to take a shower and eat, but he told she was no allowed food until the next day as she was told. He said rules are rules and you learned to do as told or end up in the ravine food for the animals.

That night he could no longer hold back his urges and went to rape Kelly. She was too weak to fight him and when it was all over she asked Bertha for away to kill herself. Bertha said even if there was a way she would not help her. Bertha's face showed what happens when you don't follow the rules.

Kelly could not get out of bed the next day. He liked having an ex-virgin around so he let her stay in bed and made Bertha work the garden in her place. Bertha now hated the little white girl even more. He was letting her break rules that she was never allowed to break. Bertha did not realize it but she was jealous of Kelly. After a month of doing as told Kelly had been raped to many times to remember, but then realized she was now pregnant. She kept on working trying to think of a way to kill herself and his monster of a baby.

After two months Bertha noticed that Kelly had not had a period and asked if Kelly was ok. Kelly said no and would Bertha please help her get rid of the baby before he found out. Bertha thought if there is a baby she would end up taking care of it and she wanted no part of it. She told Kelly that in the tool shed was some fertilizer if she could get some of it and eat it she would abort the baby. She would become very sick and would not be able to work; she would feel his belt on top of it all. Kelly stated she did not care she could not bring his monster into the world. Bertha asked how she knew it was a monster. Kelly said what else it could be coming from his loins.

It took several days before she finally had time to get to the fertilizer and stuff handfuls in her mouth. Bertha watched her and said stop you will kill yourself as well as the baby, Kelly replied that's what she wanted to do.

Kelly took two days to die after her miscarriage.

He took her remains and tossed them in the ravine he never knew about the baby. Bertha was not sure he even knew how to make babies.

It was time for number three.

CHAPTER EIGHT

E HAD TO think up what to do because young white girls were not tough enough for what he needed. He picked a small farm town this time hoping for a good old farm girl.

He left the next morning right after breakfast and drove for three hours to get to the town he wanted. Here he pulled the same routine as before, only this time waiting in the farmers market for one to come by. He saw a young dark black woman that was moving crates and boxes of fruit and vegetables around with no problem. She was what he wanted, but how to get her to his van was a problem. Then it finally dawned on him that all he had to do was buy a crate of fruit and she would load it into his van for him. So he walked up to her with a limp and asked how much a crate of oranges were and once she told him he said I'll buy a crate if you will load it in my van for me. As she took the crate to his van he asked what her name was, she answered Lilly. As she put the crate in the van she noticed it was padded and asked what he used it for. He pushed her in and said this is what while pointing the gun at her. He said give me your cell phone which she did. Lilly was one to put up a fight, but not with a gun so all she could do was fuss and fume to herself inside her padded cell. She stayed awake the whole trip and when he backed into the yard and locked the gate behind him she was ready for him. When he opened the van door Lilly jumped out trying to land on him, but instead hit the ground since he was standing to the side. Lilly then jumped up running. He did not try to stop her; his two hunting dogs would find her.

These dogs he kept chained in the woods and let no one near them, because he did not want anyone making friends with them. Their names where Buddy and Sissy, they were German Shepherds.

What he did not know was that when he let them run lose at night so they could get some exercise, they would come to the bunkhouse after the lights were out and they would feed them the left over's. If he ever found out he would kill the dogs and throw their bodies into the ravine, then get a new set. All of us would take a beaten for it too.

When he heard the dogs howling he knew she was treed, and when he found the dogs he found Lilly under a fallen tree hidden by overgrowth. He pulled her out by her hair. He told her to strip out of her cloths and when she refused he took his belt to her. One strike and Lilly did as told.

Once Lilly was naked he could not hold back on his sexual needs. He told the dogs to heal and he attacked her there and then taking her in every hole possible. Once done with her he told her to start back to the house with his juices running down her legs. He and the dogs followed. He gave Lilly a head start so he could watch her backside as they climbed the mountain. He told her the rules as they climbed the mountain back up. She stopped long enough to ask why her and he told her because he wanted her and that was all he would say.

All Lilly could think about was what he did to her and the mess running down her legs. She wanted to get cleaned up as soon as possible she felt so dirty. She slowed down on the hard slope and he told her to speed up or he was ready to take her again. Lilly almost ran all the way back.

They went by the dog yard and hooked the dogs back up. He told her to never come near the dogs he didn't want them to become pets. He fed and watered them every day.

Once back at the bunkhouse he told Bertha to train Lilly.

Lilly was so mad because there was not a thing she could do about the situation she was in and there was no one to miss her. Her boss would think she got mad over what some customer said and just quit. Someone would steal her car and it would be was if she never existed.

Things settled down into a routine once Lilly was part of his team of women. Bertha would fix the meals three times a day and keep the bunkhouse clean. Lilly worked the vegetable garden and he worked in the pot garden.

Once all the vegetables were picked and canned it was time to harvest the pot and fix it so he could sell it. He sold it from his van when he sold the vegetables. He had been doing this for years and knew his customers and would not sell to anyone he did not know. He told his customers if they wanted to have someone new to have what he sold he would sell it them and they could pass it on. This way he stayed safe.

The girls could relax for a couple of months as winter came on or so they thought.

CHAPTER NINE

ONCE THE WEATHER got to cold for the girls to go outside naked, they thought they would have it made with nothing to do except to lie around or play games. Lilly helped Bertha because she took her place when she could not work. When it was that time of the month or he had decided to hurt one of them so bad they could not work. He would get mad for no reason and whip one of them until he could not raise his arm anymore.

I think it went back to his childhood when he was beaten so much, but who knows what goes on in someone like that's mind.

Then one morning in late September he came in carrying ski suits. He stated that Lilly would help gather wood for the cook stove because that was the only source of heat for the bunkhouse. He would not put electric heat in the bunkhouse because it would run up his electric bill and someone might notice and he did not need anybody snooping around.

This would happen once or twice a week until the snow got too deep to get to the wood, which was on the side of mountain they had not been too. He had bought a four-wheeler and trailer to haul out the wood. Lilly would load and unload what he cut down and split. If there was enough daylight and they did not stop for sex they could get about 10 loads per day. This is a lot of work for the one woman, but they were in good physical shape.

One night when there was a light snow the dogs came to the bunkhouse after lights out and they felt sorry for them out in the cold and let them in sleep by the woodstove. They thought they would get the dogs out before he came to breakfast, but it snowed a little during the night and once the dogs were let out their tracks were in the new snow only coming from the bunkhouse. He was not real smart but he knew about animals and tracking.

He was really furious when he came in, he told both women to turn around so he could whip them. Lilly begged him to let the dogs live, that they were not spoiled, but being kept safe from the cold, that they would still do his bidding. She said beat them all he wanted but please don't harm the dogs they were not at fault. He thought about it for a couple of minutes and then to their surprise he said ok that she had a point. Beside he was hungry and wanted to eat instead of beating two dumb women. The two women thanked him over and over while they ate breakfast.

The winter months fell into a quiet time of healing and wonderings. The women had a lot of time on their hands and minds. They had nothing to give or celebrate.

Around Christmas both women became sad and each in turn talked about their families.

Bertha said the father of her three boys ran away right after the third one was born. He was a handsome man and a lady chaser. The youngest one is Joseph now three, next is Bryan five, and the oldest James seven years old. The boys are probably living with her mother and father who are in their fifties. She misses the big family Christmas they would be having, including her two sisters and three brothers. She wonders if she will ever see them again.

Lilly had no family to talk about, since she lost her parents and siblings in a house fire when she was four years old. Once old enough to leave her aunt who was so mean to her, she was gone. All her Christmas's were spent in her room with no presents or anything. While her Aunt June drank away the day.

She usually worked the bar or restaurants on Christmas day. Now setting there with Bertha she said she would have done things differently. If she ever got out of there she would have a big Christmas party every year.

CHAPTER TEN

JANUARY AND FEBRUARY had too much snow for them to get any wood. But come March the snow let up and they began the hard work of hauling and stacking the wood.

One day as they were loading the trailer Lilly slipped and tumbled down the mountain side. When he got to her she was banged up and had a broken leg. He wanted to throw her in the ravine since they were closer to it than the bunkhouse. Lilly talked and talked to him trying to make him see he would lose a good worker if he did. He said there were no drugs or medicine for her. Lilly said yes there was the pot that would help with the pain and she would set the leg for herself with a wood splint.

He said Lilly would be a hardship on Bertha but he would let Bertha decide if it would be. He said ok he would get the trailer as close as he could and then he could load her on it.

Once in the bunkhouse Bertha said it would be no trouble to take care of her. They put her in bed and she did the best she could do.

It was a few days later when Lilly asked Bertha if she thought the fall had hurt the baby. Bertha said what baby and how far along was she. Lilly said about a month maybe six weeks. Bertha said are you planning on keeping it? Lilly said of course she was raised to keep it. Bertha said this is different, I am a Christian woman but his babies should never be born. They would be deformed worse than he is and probably a whole lot meaner. She said don't let him know you are pregnant or he would throw you and your baby in the ravine to die. Lilly said what do I do, I want to keep this baby no matter what? Bertha said if you won't abort the monster then you will pay the price when he notices your condition. Lilly said how do you know he will do this, Bertha just said mark my words. No more was said about the baby for now.

He said since Lilly was laid up he would have to get one or two more women, because it was time to get ready for planting, and taking care of both the gardens again.

CHAPTER ELEVEN

H E SET OUT the next day for a town in the North Carolina Mountains.

He did his usual thing of waiting in a grocery store parking, he never used Wal Mart or other big box stores because their security was too tight. It did not take long for a woman to come along and ask if she could help. She was on the way to her car when she saw him leaning on his van looking very lost. She left her cart and walked over to him and asked if she could help and he said yes she could get in the back of the van and showed her his gun, she did as told but she screamed for help first. He locked the door and on his way to the driver side he got her purse out of the cart.

He had decided to get one woman at a time because it was a whole lot safer, as this time showed. When Mary screamed a little old lady a couple of cars down saw what was happening and told police she saw his face. She gave the police the information about what he looked like and it looked like a monster to them so they did not believe her. They could do no more because of the thousands of white vans out there.

CHAPTER TWELVE

HE GOT OUT of town and back home in record time afraid he was being chased. Once back home he told this one called Mary the same things as all the others and took her to the bunkhouse where the women were having lunch.

Mary is a school teacher, white, 42 years old about out 5' 4" tall. She never married, because the school children were her life. She dated every now and then but not recently. Her father was dead and her mother in an old folk's home. She was scared to death and could hardy talk. Because she had never been naked in front of anyone in her life she was very embarrassed. The girls told her she would get used to it all. Since this would be her first day in the sun they said she could work the pot garden, she had to ask what a pot garden was, where the sun wasn't so hot. When she was told about the sex she screamed no, no, no way and they said yes, yes, yes the most brutal and degrading kind there was.

He came and ate lunch then took the new woman to the garden. Pushing her around and yelling she was so stupid. He slapped her once so hard she fell to the ground crying, they forgot to tell her this is what he liked. So while she was down he took her right then and there. She was a virgin and once he found out she became his favorite until the next one came along. She would not get up when he was done and he whipped her and sent her back to the bunkhouse. There were only a couple of hours of daylight left in the day anyway.

At supper that night he said he would be gone again tomorrow to find another woman. For Bertha to work the vegetable garden and Mary the pot garden and they better do a good job or when he got back they would get the belt.

Mary cried all night and he listened outside the bunkhouse and smiled his evil smile while doing his evil thing.

CHAPTER THIRTEEN

THIS TIME HE wanted something different, a different type of woman. He had been watching TV and decided he wanted some foreign pussy.

He decided to get a Vietnamese woman just to have something that might be a lot of fun. He was tired of the stupid and whiny white and black women.

He set out the next morning very early about four in the morning. He drove for about six hours to get to the small town where he thought he could find what he was looking for. He found it in a small strip mall, one with a nail salon in it. He would wait tell closing time around 9 o'clock that evening to make his move. He found a large shopping mall and pulled in to rest up, because he would have a long night time drive home.

At 8:45 pm he woke and headed to the salon, (which he had found on the internet). There was only one car at the end of parking lot where the shop was and he saw the woman locking up. He pulled his van in front of her car so she had to pass in front of the van. He stopped and got out asking if she knew where a certain place was, she said no and tried to get past him to her car, that's when he pulled out the gun and told her to get in the back of the van or he would shot her.

She did as she was told once in the van he took her purse and asked for her cell phone, she said she did not have it, it was in the purse. For some reason he did not believe her and slapped her hard enough to knock her out and then he searched her for and found it in her pocket.

He started the long drive home happy as a man like him could be. Once home he woke up his captive and asked her for her name. She spoke in Vietnamese and he could not understand a word. He shook her and said to speak in English. She said my name is Tai please tell what is happening.

He then told her to take off her clothes but she refused and he hit her again and again until she was knocked out again. He then took her clothes off and carried her to the bunkhouse and dumped her on a cot.

The others where awake from the moment he'd backed in the gate. He said get her ready to work in the morning cutting wood.

The girls just cleaned her wounds and covered her with blankets to sleep till morning. Then they went back to bed.

Early in the morning Tai awoke and the whole nightmare came back as a sudden and painful memory. Tai began to cry and the women got up and set with her. Telling her that he meant every word he said and she should not upset him in anyway because he was very mean.

Tai is a 5'5" slender 31 year old, light brown skin woman with long black hair worn in a ponytail.

Tai told them who she was and what she did for a living. She said she had two children one boy Kevin Jr. nine years old and Little Tai two years old. That she was born in America from parents born here. Her grandparents came from Vietnam while the US was fighting there and because of others like them found work and were happy here. Her grandmother could only have one child that was Tai's mother, who went on to marry an American named Bill. Her grandparents were gone now both having died from cancer.

What can I do my family will be so worried? They said there is nothing anyone can do; he covers his tracks too well. It was time for her to eat and get ready to help cut wood. She said I know nothing about cutting wood, you will before the day is over and you better learn fast.

They told her about the ski suits they would wear when they worked outside in the winter but once spring and summer came no cloths were allowed. No cloths were allowed inside the bunkhouse at anytime.

Tai stated he is a very sick man and the women said tell us something we don't already know.

Her first breakfast was very hard and she wanted to cry but did not because they told her how he liked to see and hear them cry.

Once dressed for the outside Mary and Tai set out with him to the woods, with the dogs following along. Mary told her all they had to do was keep the trailer loaded with wood as fast as he could cut it up. Once the trailer was full he would drive the gator back to the bunkhouse where they would unload. If Tai was not afraid of a little hard work she should be ok.

They worked for hours getting a lot of wood, because he said a late March snow was on its way and they could be snowed in for weeks. Tai tried to keep her end up, but Mary had to work double so he would not get angry and hurt them both. They were not allowed to talk so it wasn't until after suppertime that Tai could thank Mary for her hard work.

The next day he wanted only Tai to help with the wood he said they did not need to get that much. It was a warm day and once in the woods with her he could not wait for her to strip and give him a blow job without biting him.

This meant he would have to hurt her a lot so she would know he meant it when he said he would. So he started by raping her, beating her, pinching her nipples, whatever it took to get what he wanted.

But Tai had taken a course on what to do and not do when being raped. She was told to just go limp and not scream for it would give them what they wanted. But those people did not him and what he was capable of. For doing this only made him mad and he hurt her even more.

Tai was no good for work when he was done with her. So he took her back to the bunkhouse and told her to be ready for work in the morning or go to the ravine.

Meanwhile back at the garden Kelly was working the food garden and Mary was working the pot garden. When Mary heard Lilly cry out and ran to see what was wrong. Lilly had miscarriage the baby now three months old. Mary knew enough that if he found out he would kill Lilly. She told Lilly to get back in the bunkhouse and if he asked what was wrong, to tell him she had just gotten her period. Mary took the thing that was supposed to be a baby to the ravine and got rid of it.

That night the women tried to figure out a way to destroy the babies as they came along and before he found out.

It seemed Bertha had no problem because in the whole time she had been there she had not gotten pregnant. She said there was the old fashion way of sticking something up there and they would miscarriage that way, but they could bleed to death if not careful. They made a pact to help each other when their times came.

CHAPTER FOURTEEN

H E TOLD THE girls to keep the shovels in the bunkhouse because of the snow storm coming. He said they were calling for 6" to 12" and they would have to shovel a path to the wood pile for the stove. That night the girls kept the dogs and the shovels inside. When they went to sleep there was no snow on the ground but come morning there was at least a foot of the white stuff.

Mary and Tai put on the ski suits and shoveled a path to the wood shed. They were just finishing up when he yelled for them to dig a path to his house. The path to his house would be three times as long as the one to the wood shed. He shot at them and yelled they better do it if they did not want the whip when he got to them. They yelled they would do it but they had to warm up first. An hour later they started on the path to his house, the snow was wet and heavy. It took almost two more hours to get it done. Once they reached the steps he said to hold up he was going back with them to get breakfast, which Bertha had hot and ready knowing he would be there. She was pretty sure he could not cook.

He told them at breakfast that until the snow was gone they could take it easy, that the only thing he would want was sex and they could take turns.

He said once he could get out he was going to get two more girls, because come spring he was going to enlarge the two gardens. With one woman always laid up he wanted two to work the food garden and two to work the pot garden. So they had about two weeks of just satisfying his needs which could be hell at times. He decided that it was time to get a threesome going with different ones on different nights. The women did not like this but what else could they do.

One morning after breakfast once he was gone they set down to try and figure away to get away from him. They were not allowed on the back porch and they could not figure out how he carried a key in the summer when he was naked. But yet he would mess with the lock and unlock it, the same thing when he locked it. They drew plans of how to jump him when he came in the bunkhouse, or when he was having sex with one of them but not knowing how to unlock the back door left them with no way out. There were no windows on the back porch and the rest of the windows were ten feet off the ground. They gave up and threw the pieces of paper in the trash.

A couple of days later he came to take the trash to the ravine and throw it away. On the ride down the mountain he hit a bump and threw some of the trash out on the ground. He got out to pick it up and found one of their drawings he was mad as he could be.

When he got back to the house he got his whip and went to the bunkhouse. When he got there he threw the piece of paper on the table and said if you do anything to me you will stay here and starve. The lock on the back door is a combination lock and I am the only one who knows the combination. Now turn around and get a whipping for even thinking about it. He gave each one a couple of blows and left still mad. The women would never think of leaving again.

CHAPTER FIFTEEN

THE SNOW WAS cleared off the road so it was time to go get number five. He decided on a Mexican woman this time out for a change of flavor again. He went north this time to a place he knew where Mexicans lived. Again he did his thing at a grocery store where there were a lot of Mexican women going in and out. Most had a man with them or kids, so he waited and waited finally he decided on one with a baby, he could always get rid of the kid. When she came out she had her arms full so he offered to help speaking in Spanish. She said thank you and gave him a bag at the same time he showed her the gun and said to get in his van or he would kill her baby. She was so frightened she did not think to scream for help. Once he had her in the van he asked for her cell phone and she gave him her purse with the phone in it.

He only had a couple of hours ride home and was back before dark. Once back inside the gate he opened the van and he asked what her name was she said it was Maria. Maria was a typical Spanish woman small 5'2" and dark skinned.

Being it was so cold he was going to have her undress in the warm bunkhouse, strange for a monster until you think what he will probably do to her once there.

Once there he said give the child to one of the women and get undressed. She did not want to give up the baby so he grabbed it out of her arms and threw it to Bertha. Maria was doing his favorite thing crying. He said take off your clothes or I will kill your child and she did as told. He could not wait and took her right then and there cussing her, hurting her all in Spanish. Maria screamed in English and Spanish. Once he was done with her he put his cloths on and told Bertha to give him the baby, Maria screamed you said you would not hurt him, please give me my baby. He laughed and said you will come to know me and that know you can't trust me. I am throwing the baby in the ravine to die. It did not matter that Maria was in a lot of pain she went after him trying to get her baby back, but in the end he left with it.

He did as he promised, but he did let them know he wrung its neck first.

Maria was inconsolable Mary and Lilly tried to talk to her but all she did was cuss, scream and cry in both langues at the top of her lungs. They told her to calm down before he came back for super or he would do to her what he did to her baby. She said that she wanted to die so she could be with her baby. Lilly said if he knows you want to die he will not kill you, only make you wish you were dead. Understanding this she became quiet too quiet.

He came to supper and did not say anything much to anybody. He told them he had to go to town and get groceries in the morning and would not be back until just before supper.

Maria asked if he did kill her baby and he said yes. She began to cry again, he said you better be over this before spring or you could join him.

As the days and nights went by it was April before they knew it. He put them to plowing the fields. There was one woman pulling the plow and one following behind keeping the plow straight. It was now a two acre vegetable garden and a two acre pot field. It took the women over a week on each field even with him on them with his whip. The women were so tired at night all they did was eat and sleep. It seemed that Maria was going to be ok because she did her part without protest. She was just a little too quiet to suit the other women. Next came the planting and seeding which was even more back breaking than the plowing. Again it took the women almost two weeks to get it all done.

Once done with the planting it was time to hoe and replace plants that did not make it. He would have two women in each field but never the same two in a row because some worked better with others.

CHAPTER SIXTEEN

NOW THAT IT was spring Mary wanted to go fishing and give them something different to eat. At supper one night in late April she asked him if there was a lake somewhere on his 100 acres. He said yes just below where they cut wood. She asked if he would get some fishing equipment so they could catch supper and save him some money. He said he would think about it and it also depended on them getting their work done.

At breakfast the next morning he said he was going into town for groceries again and would be back by supper time and they better not goof off.

He returned just in time for supper but did not say anything about fishing until supper was just about over. He then stated they could go fishing tomorrow as long as they got their work done in time.

Since the time had just changed they had more time to get the work done and go fishing. He came about five that evening carrying five rod and reels. They were excited to go and have fun even with him there. They caught enough crappie and bass so that he could freeze a bunch and still have some for supper the next day. Mary and Bertha were the only ones who knew how to clean them so that's what they did that night without complaint.

That night Maria left the bunkhouse and found the lake, she was going to kill herself but then remembered that if she committed suicide she would not go to heaven to be with her baby, she would go to hell. So at the last minute she went back to the bunkhouse. She laid there trying to think of some way to get him to kill her but nothing would come to mind then.

CHAPTER SEVENTEEN

I T WAS TIME for number six so he could keep from using Bertha in the gardens. He just picked a town by sticking a pin in a map and then looking the town up on the internet.

He told the women he would leave very early in the morning and be back late that night. For them to get their work done and they could go to the lake if they wanted.

He left at two in the morning to get there around noon that day. Once there he set up as usual waiting by the van with his map and gun.

It was a while before a woman came along he liked. He picked a very petite woman with very porcelain features. She parked a few spaces up in one of the smallest cars he had ever seen. When she walked by he asked if she could help him find a street named Strange Street. She almost went on by once she saw his face, but did not want to seem insensitive.

Once she was close enough he showed the gun and said get in the van or you're dead. He took her purse as she struggled to get in the van. Being only 4'8" and scared out of her mind in was not easy for her. He finally shoved her in and slammed the door. She might be little but she was proud and refused to let herself cry or speak.

He stopped only for gas and food on the long 10 hour trip back home. Arriving around midnight he opened the van door and woke her up. He asked her name and she would not answer. He slapped her hard and still no answer. He slammed the van door and got her purse and found her license. Her name was Donna a 30 year old white woman, weighing about 93 lbs.

He opened the back of the van and said Donna take off all your clothes except your shoes, this is your new forever home. She refused to move so he grabbed her and took off her blouse, skirt, bra and panties in a very rough manner losing her shoes in the process.

Once she was naked he thought of how she looked more like a large doll than a person. He could not hold back his sexual needs. He locked her in the back of the van while he undressed. Once he got her back out and she realized what he intended she screamed and screamed. His cock was very large and she was too small and could not handle it.

The women in the bunkhouse watched in horror as he picked her up and rammed her on his cock like a doll. She was so small he made her bleed with the first stroke. Then he killed her with the next few strokes.

Once finished with her he dropped her on the ground like a used rag. He used her clothes to clean himself up and then went and got the four-wheeler and trailer, threw her body in the back and headed to the ravine.

He left the back of the van unlocked and the girls ran and got a look at her license and saw her name was Donna. This way they could at least say a prayer for her. They knew he was a monster but this was over the top for even him.

So now he would have to find another number six.

CHAPTER EIGHTEEN

H E SAW ON the news where they were putting together a lot of the missing women as a one man job.

So he decided to try a new game. He knew there were nightclubs where he could pick-up a drunken woman around closing time.

So he picked a town with the dart again and used the computer to pick a bar somewhere far off even if he had to spend the night parked on a dark lonely road on the way back.

He found a backwoods bar with nothing around for miles in either direction. He pulled into the parking lot the next night as far away from the lights as possible. It was almost closing time and he watched as the people left and the parking lot was getting empty.

Then just as he was about to give up this couple came out of the bar fighting and arguing really loud. When they got to the guys car, she refused to get in and the guy drove off without her. He called to her by name since he heard the guy call her Debbie. Debbie is a white woman about 5' 3" slender.

Debbie said what the hell do you want, he said nothing I was just leaving and heard the argument. I thought you might need a lift home. Debbie thought about it for a while, so long in fact that he said its ok I'll leave you here. Debbie realized everyone had gone and it was him or a long walk home on the lonely dark road. She said ok and thanks.

When she got to the van he said you'll have to ride in the back the front seat is broken. She got to the side of the van he showed her his gun as he opened the door. She got in without a sound, she was no longer drunk. He took her purse and locked her in.

He decided to sleep right there in the parking lot, he figured anyone seeing the van would think it was left behind or someone was sleeping it off.

He woke about 8 o'clock in the morning and checked on his catch. She needed to go to the bathroom really bad. Since he did not want the smell in his van he told her to get out and go right there beside the van. She asked what if someone came by and he said if she would shut-up and do it, it would already be done. Debbie got out pulled her red dress up and blue panties down, once done she pulled up her big girl panties and got back in the van without being told to because his gun scared her half to death.

She asked what was he going to do with her and he said you'll find out before the day is over.

He headed home thinking of all the ways he could hurt her and about halfway home he decided to find a lonely spot and take her now.

He drove some back roads until he found a side road into some woods. He got out and opened the van he told Debbie to remove her clothes and give them to him he put them up front and got undressed in front of her.

He crawled into the van with his gun and told her he wanted her now and not to try anything or he would kill her. She could see he was hard and ready.

He raped her just the once because he needed to be on the road. He gave her, her clothes to clean up with and headed home.

Debbie cried a long time before falling asleep for the rest of the trip.

It was about 11 o'clock when he parked the van at home. Too tired to give his normal speech he took Debbie direct to the bunkhouse and since the girls where awake told them to let her know the rules.

Mary set Debbie down and explained all about this being her home from now on and the work she would have to do, including the sex part.

Debbie said she already knew about the sex part that he raped her in the van on the way home. Mary said that was a first that Debbie must have made an impression on him. She said I am a 55 year old Italian widow out looking for good time. She explained what happened with her boyfriend Dale at the bar. Dale was flirting with a young blond woman and I got mad and we were fighting as we were leaving and I got stuck without a ride. Mary said you got a ride a ride straight to hell. Well he has his six women let's see how long they each last.

CHAPTER NINETEEN

HE NOW HAD six women, but one was costing him money and not working at all. His thoughts where to get rid of Lilly, then he would have his two women for each garden leaving Bertha at the bunkhouse and for back up duty.

The more he thought about it the madder he got and finally one day in late April while all of the women were busy plowing fields he pulled the four-wheeler up to the bunkhouse and before anyone knew what he was doing he strangled Lilly and put her body in the trailer for the ride to the raven with the trash.

Bertha could only stand and watch as he worked so fast there was nothing she could have done.

Since there were no screams the rest of the women would not know anything happened until lunch time.

Maria said I need to break a leg so he would kill me and I can go to heaven to be with my child. They all were very tired of hearing Maria complain.

Mary, Tai and Debbie just said a payer for Lilly. He on the other hand was happy and took Tai that night, the sick bastard.

CHAPTER TWENTY

THINGS SETTLED DOWN after Lilly's death into very hard days and nights.

Days of plowing, hoeing, planting and watering the fields made them all exhausted. To water he had long hoses run down every four or five rows. This meant dragging the heavy hose up and down the rows until all had been watered each day.

Then at the end of May and beginning of June came picking the vegetables and fruits from his peach trees. They would box up the vegetables and then clean and repack them for shipment to the Farmers Market where he sold them right off the van.

They also had to harvest his pot and package it so it was sold in packets inside the vegetables and fruit boxes. After putting so much pot down in the middle of each box of fruit and vegetables they would mark the box with an I or II depending on how much pot was in each box. The ones he sold to were told not to open the boxes until they left the market. Some threw away the vegetables or fruit just to get to his superior pot.

This went on until the end of October until time for the pumpkins.

The women formed a chain and passed the pumpkins up to the bunkhouse to be washed. Tai said she knew how to paint the pumpkins so they would sell better and Debbie said she could do it too. So he bought them the paints and brushes they would need.

Come the end of October he would use Mary and Debbie one day to get wood, the Tai and Maria the next. He told them they were calling for an early and very cold winter, so they would need to get the wood shed filled twice over before then.

This is when Maria realized she was pregnant with one of his monsters. She was about four months along and did not tell anyone. She wanted him to work her to death so she would miscarriage and die. The other women thought she might me pregnant but could not be sure, they tried to talk to Maria but she would not listen.

The working did not cause a miscarriage and by December she was showing. He asked her what was wrong he could feel something inside her when they had sex and it was not right.

She finally told him she was carrying his baby and he went ballistic. He yelled he did not want kids and if she had the child he would kill it like the last one. Maria said why don't you kill us both now and get it over with. He said you were a very good worker and I don't want to lose you. She said then I will become a sorry worker from now on. He grabbed her and began shaking her until she screamed in pain and said the baby was coming. He threw her down and set on her saying you will lose the baby and stay alive. Maria cried out in so much pain and then her water broke and the baby was on the floor for all to see.

It was deformed with no hands and feet way to small for its body. Its body was twisted unnaturally; its face looked as if someone had smashed it into a million pieces that healed all wrong. It was dead on arrival.

He screamed at Maria you bitch you had a monster, it's your entire fault and you and the monster will both die.

He beat Maria to death with his fist. While the other women stood there in shock. Once done he told them if any of them got pregnant the same would happen to them. He then took both the baby's and Maria's bodies to the ravine.

Mary finally said for whatever reasons the rest of us don't get pregnant it's a blessing.

When he came back he said that's one less mouth to feed this winter and I won't replace her till spring.

CHAPTER TWENTY ONE

L IFE SETTLED DOWN into nothing but long days and nights of playing games, eating, sleeping and sex whenever and however he wanted it.

The weather turned very cold by Christmas. The women all set around and remembered their families and their past Christmas.

It was Bertha's second Christmas and she missed her family even more than the last one. She told the other women that he didn't let them observe Christmas and that at the last one they all set around and talked about their families and what they did for the holidays.

Bertha talked about her boys—James now eight, Bryan now six and Joseph now four. Telling of how hard it was to have a Christmas with just her salary for support. But somehow she would manage at least one toy each. The boys were good boys they never complained. The grandparents always made sure the boys got presents. Bertha's parents gave gifts; her ex-husband parents lived far away in California and had little to do with her or her children.

She told Mary, Tia and Debbie about the big family Christmas with the whole family getting together aunts, uncles, cousins, bother and sisters everyone at her parents big old two story house. She would tell about the decorating of the tree on Christmas Eve and opening the presents on Christmas day. Life was really good back then and she was happy her parents would raise the boys.

Mary said she enjoyed Christmas with her students most of all. They would decorate the classroom and tell stories of Christmas. They drew names and made small presents for each other.

Mary's parents where very old and didn't make a big to do about Christmas anymore. Mary being an only child got whatever she wanted growing up and when Christmas came it was joyless for her. That's why she tried to make it as joyful as possible for her students.

Tai said her parents did not believe in Christmas for many years they stayed with their old country's religion. Until the first Christmas with

Bill who observed Christmas once they were married she decided to live under all her husband's American customs.

Tai broke down at this point and could not carry on, she tried to cry quietly so as not to upset the rest of the women.

Debbie said her family was like Bertha's having been from a large family herself. She was the only one of five sisters and brothers to have just one child. Carol was now 30 years old and expecting her first child. Debbie wished she could be there for the birth, it was due in January and was to be a boy. They would name him James Arthur after both of his grandfathers.

Debbie and her husband Adam would have a quiet Christmas together until Carol their only child came along. It was a different ballgame because Carol even from a very young age would have long list of things she wanted. She would only get a few of the items on her list and seemed happy.

They would go to his parents on Christmas Eve and enjoy a large family dinner like Bertha. Then on Christmas day they would go to her parents which would be just the five of them. Since her parents had disowned her brother and his family because they thought their lifestyle to wild for their taste.

Debbie saw her brother and his family sometime during the holidays for she was not above having hillbillies for family.

When Debbie lost her husband of 35 years to cancer she thought the world had ended. For awhile she would not go out nor have visitors. Until her brother came and made her come live with them for a couple of weeks. After that experience she was ready to see the world. She was on a cruise when she meant Dale and had begun to care about him. But since he dumped her in the parking lot and that's how she ended up here she didn't think she cared about him anymore.

Thus this was how Christmas was spent. They asked him why he never mentioned it. He said all he ever got for Christmas was beatings so he did not want anything to do with it.

The next couple of months were boring each woman lost in her own thoughts.

CHAPTER TWENTY TWO

WITH LILLY GONE he only had four women and he needed five when planting season started.

Come March he again throws the dart and this time he must make a two day trip again. He never says where he is going when he gets his victims. I don't know why and I am not going to ask.

This trip meant he would have to stop and get food for both of them and let the woman take a leak. So he plotted his route on back roads so it would easier to find places to let her pee.

This time was like the last another bar pick-up. He would arrive after a day's travel pick-up a woman around closing and start back after a nap in the parking lot like before.

The woman was a light skinned black woman about 5'7" tall about 30 lbs overweight and she came out alone looking for her car. He asked if he could help and she said she was driving a yellow Chevy rag top. He pulled his gun and said let's get in my white Chevy van. She was deathly afraid of guns and went along with him. He asked her what her name was and she said Carol. He took her purse and he could see by the skin tight blue dress and black leather cowboy boots she did not have a cell phone on her. Once locked up tight he took his nap, but during the night a cop came by and told him he would have to move on, so without any trouble his did.

This was about 3 o'clock in the morning he drove a few miles down the road and stopped to check on Carol and found her fast asleep, but she had vomited all over the inside of his van. He was so mad he woke her up and rubbed her face in it. Then told her when he found a service station she was going to clean it up. She was so hung over she didn't care what he said or did.

He drove for about an hour before finding an all night service station. He went in and bought the stuff to clean up the mess with. The guy behind the counter said awful early to be cleaning. So he told him the truth that his date had gotten sick in the back of the van and she was going to clean it up. He asked if it was alright to do it in the parking lot and the guy said yea, sure.

He moved the van to the far edge of the parking lot and got Carol awake and told her to clean-up. Carol started but she got sick again and he told her to do it in the trash bag. She just made it and once done tie the bag closed. She finished cleaning but once done she told him she had to go to the bathroom. He said I'll take you to the bathroom but you have to act like my girlfriend or you'll wait until I find a place along the road. She agreed knowing he would have gun at all times.

She went to the bathroom with no purse and no way to leave a message for help. Once she was done it was back to the van. She wondered what he was going to do with her and all the horror stories she had seen on TV came flashing back.

On the road again he knew he would not get back until around midnight so he planned to stop for lunch and skip breakfast. He knew Carol was still too sick to eat yet.

Around noon he stopped at a hamburger joint and ordered for two. He got hamburgers, fries and drinks. He gave Carol hers and by now she was starving. She asked him what he was planning to do with her and knowing her fear he just said you'll find out before morning. Now Carol was even more upset and scared stiff, just as he wanted her to be.

It was hard for Carol to sleep but a few hours from his place she finally did.

Once home he did his routine of telling her to take off her clothes and telling her this would be her home from now on. He took her to the bunkhouse and woke Bertha and told her to tell Carol the rules before she went to bed.

Once Carol knew the rules she took a shower and then cried herself to sleep.

The next morning Carol got to meet Mary, Tai and Debbie.

Carol told them she was a 44 year old divorced woman, no kids, she was born with no way to have kids. He mother was dead and her father smothered her with whatever she wanted. She was a lab tech for a large pharmacy.

Mary said it still being only March and they were calling for a long cold hard winter there was nothing much to do except play games and have sex whenever he wanted it.

Carol asked how bad would it be and they told her he had a very large dick and he liked it all the different ways she could think of.

CHAPTER TWENTY THREE

THIS YEAR LIKE the year before he had the women start the clearing out of the old garden and plowing to get it ready for planting. With such a hard winter it would take a lot more effort to get the soil ready. This year he decided to add fertilizer to both of the gardens. This meant the women would have to spread it by hand, using 5 gallon buckets and a scoop to spread it. The ground was still hard from the winter freeze and made it twice as hard on the women.

This time of year was so hard for the women, because all they wanted by the end of the day was supper, a shower and to bed to sleep. But he would come in to have his sex just about every night, sometimes two women at once or two in one night. He was very loud when he was having sex that no one got any rest until he was gone.

They asked him to try and not be so loud so they could get some rest. All he did was get louder the next time around.

How the women endured his humping them night after night is mind blowing. These were very strong women and having never meant before they became a close family of five.

CHAPTER TWENTY FOUR

T HIS YEAR AND the next went pretty much the same until winter of the second year. It was the worse winter yet with feet of snow. The women were stuck inside with little or nothing to do. By December tempers were very short. So one night when he came to the bunkhouse he wanted Tai for a partner, she was not willing so he forced her down and tried to have sex anyway. Tai struggled until she got loose and from her bed she pulled a dinner knife and cut him. He went berserk and took the knife away from her and shoved it in her heart killing her instantly.

He took Tai body outside and left it in the snow until spring when he could take it to the raven. The women were more scared of him than ever.

CHAPTER TWENTY FIVE

This March the roads were very icy a lot so he decided to find a replacement for Tai somewhere local this time.

He knew of a local old county store where he might pick-up a good strong country woman. He drove there and started doing business there so as not to cause anyone to wonder what he was up to. He found out that the store was owned by an elderly Spanish couple and their granddaughter. The couple was in their sixties and the granddaughter was nineteen years old. After a couple of weeks of not seeing any woman he might want he decided to take Patricia the young granddaughter who was strong and smart about 5'2" tall pretty body. One afternoon when he went to the store she was alone and no customers where in the store so he got his gun and told Patricia to get in his van or he would kill her and her family. He was there and gone in less than ten minutes.

The grandparents returned five minutes after they were gone to find her missing. They called the police and opened a missing person file on her, but they needed to go home because a very bad snow storm was coming. The police watched until the grandparents locked up and left. They said the girl probably ran off with one of the customers.

By this time he was home and he took Patricia to the bunkhouse and had her undress. He was so excited over someone new that he raped her then and there. Patricia was a virgin and he hurt her really bad. Once done he told Bertha to clean her up and tell her the rules.

Patricia was so badly hurt that Bertha thought that she would never make it. Bertha told him to leave her alone and let her heal or he would kill her too.

Patricia told them the details of her life that her parents were dead from an auto accident and she had been living with her grandparents since she was three years old. Being all that her grandparents had it would likely kill them with her missing.

It took Patricia several days to start to get her health back. Once she was ok they told her about the farming and that she would have to pull her own weight. Patricia said no problem with the work it was the sex that was so bad.

He came for her in a couple of weeks, raping her and causing more bleeding. It seemed the bleeding turned him on. He kept at her over the next couple of months until he hurt her to the point that she would never get pregnant.

CHAPTER TWENTY SIX

OVER THE NEXT five years things went well for him. The women became strong and hard. Each year bringing Bertha, Mary, Debbie, Carol and Patricia very close together.

It had been seven years since Debbie was brought there and she was hoeing the vegetable garden one day when she stepped on a snake and it bit her. She screamed and Mary who was her partner that day came running. When she saw what had happened she ran to get him in the pot garden.

He came as fast as he could on his four wheeler and cut the wound and sucked out the poison. He then put her on the four wheeler and took her to Bertha to take care of. Bertha put a potion on the wound in hopes of drawing out more of the poison. It turned out that Debbie was allergic to snake venom. It took Debbie two days to die of the poison and she was blotted and hardly recognizable.

He came and took her body to the ravine. He said he would put out something to keep the snakes away. But the women refused to go back to the fields until he got them some garden boots to wear. At first he said no way but after thinking on it he said ok. He got the women's shoe sizes and went shopping. Buying some here and some there so no one would ask him too many questions about buying five pairs of boots. He bought one pair for himself and four pairs for the women. He would buy a pair for the new women as soon as he got her.

CHAPTER TWENTY SEVEN

SINCE IT HAD been nearly five and half years since he had to go on the hunt he hoped things had settled down. He hoped that they were not looking for the white van killer anymore. It helped that he bought a blue van a couple of years before. He felt he could go back to throwing the dart at the map and find a good place to hunt.

This time it landed near the coast and he was glad because he had never been there before. He picked a tourist town where he might not be remembered. This would be a four day round trip. So he made sure the women had all they needed and left early the next morning.

He enjoyed the long drive seeing the dairy farms and the cotton fields. He said to himself not to wait so long to get out of the house and see the world.

Once at the coast he drove around looking for a place to pick-up a woman. There were a lot of tourist traps but no large stores, so he decided to try women leaving the beach. Two women were walking holding hands and kissing. He could tell which one was supposed to be the man and decided then he wanted her. He wanted to show her want a woman really needs. He watched them for a while until they split up for some reason. The manly woman went home and the woman went shopping.

Once at the women's place he saw that it was dark around where they had to park their cars. When he saw the manly woman get out of the car he jumped out of his van and ran up to her and put the gun to her head. He made her get in the van and he removed her cell phone. He told her it was going to be a long ride and she better co-operate.

He looked on her license and saw her name was Erin, a white woman, thirty five years old with dark black hair cut short and a very trim body.

The trip back was uneventful Erin behaved herself because she hated guns. Since her brother was killed twenty year ago by a drive by shooter.

Once back at the bunkhouse he took her right there on the floor.

He left her hurt and bleeding, for she had never had a real man before, especially not one as big as he was.

Bertha again took over Erin's care and said she would get better over time but her mind would never be the same. She told Bertha that her partner was named Sandra and they had been together twenty years since high school. She said Sandra would be devastated once she found out that she was gone. From then on she did as told but kept to herself.

CHAPTER TWENTY EIGHT

T HE SPRING COMES early this year, Bertha has been here now eleven years and time seems to fly by.

This year he wants to enlarge his crops to include blackberries, raspberries and strawberries. He has the women plant the bushes full of green berries so in a month they will have a large crop of all three.

This planting is not easy in the rocky soil. They have to remove large rocks by hand and he takes them in the four wheeler to the ravine.

But the planting gets done after two weeks of hard labor in the fields and the bed. He never lets up with the sex no matter how hard he has worked.

He has been watching sex on the internet and now is trying new and weird positions with the very tried and unwilling women.

Somehow the women keep going thru the spring, summer and fall.

When winter sets in again Erin is very unhappy and not wanting to live. Her mood has gotten worse over the past months because she could not find any way to escape. She hates him for using her as a woman and not the man she always wanted to be. By Christmas she is so down she hardy eats anything and is sick a lot of the time. Just after Christmas they have a high snowfall of several feet and are shut down for a couple of days. This means he can't get to them until they shovel a path for him. They take their time so they get a reprieve from sex.

One morning they wake up and find Erin gone. They suit up and follow her footsteps in the snow and find her frozen to death not far from the bunkhouse. She at last had her freedom from him.

He leaves her body in the snow until he can get the four wheeler to the ravine.

CHAPTER TWENTY NINE

A S ALWAYS HE waits till March to get ready to find another victim.

He decides to find a town with a laundry mat and see what he can pick up there. A look on the internet finds just what he is looking for and not far away.

He goes out and steals a tag off a van to replace his temporarily. This method has worked so far and he hopes it keeps working. He knows that at least a time or two his van has shown up on parking lot camera footage. But by the time they find it he has already changed it back to the right tag.

He tries to plan so as not to give the police much to go on. Like changing the tags and changing from a white van to a new blue one.

He even went back a couple of times to the store where he got Patricia to check how the police were doing. Patricia's grandparents said the police believe she ran away with a customer and not looking for her. In a couple of months the store was closed and the grandparents gone leaving him no chance of getting caught.

He will only be gone a day at most for this pick-up. He takes some old clothes too wash just to fit in.

As the afternoon turns into night a woman shows up with a lot of laundry to do. Once she gets the clothes in the washers she notices him in a corner by himself. She needs to talk to someone about her bad day, so without getting close to him she tells him her name is Barbara a housewife and mother of two girls, Sophie 15 and Beth 17 years old. Her husband Ralph is out of town with his job and the washer broke down and it is wash day. So she takes the girls to ball practice and comes here. She has to get the clothes done by the time practice is over so she can pick the girls up. Beth can't drive yet having failed her driving test.

She has not taken a close look at him until now when he puts his cloths in the dryer and she sees the bad side of his face. She realizes that she should not have told him she was alone. When he shows her his gun and says be quiet if you want to live, she is quiet.

He takes her to his van and takes her purse and cell phone. He heads home happy he has found a white woman who looks healthy and strong.

It's dark when he gets back, he tells her to get out the van and head to the bunkhouse.

Once there he has her remove her clothes after he has to slap her around a couple of times. He looks her over and decides to take her later, he is tired and wants to be in peak form when takes her.

Bertha and the other women fill Barbara in on what the rules are and what could be happening later that night.

Barbara worries more about her girls than she does about herself. The girls will be all alone at the school not knowing what has happened and they could get hurt by some crazy like him.

He comes back that night and takes Barbara in ways she never dreamed of. She is left bloodied and hurting. She has been fixed so she can't have children but he stills has left her damaged inside.

Bertha takes care of her but Barbara won't be able to do much for a few days until she heals.

By planting time Barbara is ready to work her share of the gardens because Bertha and the others have helped her cope with all that is happening.

What Barbara does not know and will never know is that the girls called their father when they can't get their mother and he is in bed with another woman. The girls call a cab to take them home very upset by everything that has happened. When their father gets home they go to the laundry mat and find their car but no Barbara or their clothes. Someone has stolen their clothes and their mother. They call the police and they take out a missing person report, but because she is a grown woman and no one has seen her that's all they can do. So he gets away with it again.

CHAPTER THIRTY

THE NEXT COUPLE of years go by with little or no problems. He takes his produce to the market and comes home very happy by the money his had made. Selling the pot with the produce nets him three to four thousand dollars a day. He keeps all his cash in the house in a gun safe. He has more money than he needs to get by, but he loves to count the money all the time.

Then on a spring morning Mary gets up from a rough night and puts her boots on without looking inside. She feels a couple of bites on her foot and once she gets the boot off realizes there is a Black Widow spider in there that has bitten her several times.

She screams for help and he comes running being halfway there to get breakfast. Again he cuts the wounds and sucks out the poison. Bertha takes over but it likes very bad right off. The poison is spreading up Mary's leg fast. Mary did not know she was allergic to spiders.

Mary went into a coma and her leg turned black. They could cut her leg off and maybe save her. But he said she would be no good to him with one leg to let her die. Which she did a couple of days later. He then took her body to the ravine.

CHAPTER THIRTY ONE

IT WAS THE middle of growing season and he was going to need a replacement real quick.

He decided the laundry mat was the best place to pick up a woman. So he threw a dart at the map again and then went online to find the right place in town. There are not many laundry mats anymore and some are secured with cameras. He finally found one in seedy part of town that would do.

He left the next morning and would be gone two days. Leaving the women to keep the gardens up, the vegetables picked and the pot taken care of.

Once on the road he found a freedom he only felt when away from home. He thought many times about to just keep going for he had enough money to do it. Over time the women would die and no one would know what had happened there. He always did what he had to do and came back home.

He found the laundry mat and parked outside. He took some old rags inside and threw them in the washer. He was alone to start with it being early in the morning. About an hour later a woman and her two children came in. He started talking to the kids before the mother stopped them from talking to strangers. She later apologized to him saying you have to teach them young. He asked the names of her kids and she said they are my grandkids Denise and Lucia. Their father is my son Jerry. They live with me my name is Amy and my husband is Albert. He told her she did not look old enough to have grandkids. She said she was 47 years old going on 90. They both laughed at that.

Once she had the clothes in the washers, the kids wanted to go to the store next door for a drink. She said no she did not have money for drinks. He said let me buy them a drink, Amy said ok but for them to come right back.

He made his move as soon as the kids were in the store. He showed her his gun and said get in the van real quiet like or he would hurt her grandkids when they came back. Amy did as told, she had no purse or cell phone to take, just loose change in a pocket for the dryers.

This time when he got home he told Amy to take off her clothes and put on Mary's boots to start work in the garden right away because they were behind. He needed his van loaded and ready for in the morning.

He pushed her down to where Carol was working and told Carol to put her to work and explain the rules as they worked. Carol told Amy this was to be her home for the rest of her life and that working these fields and being there for him when he wanted sex was all there was to know and do.

Amy found out first hand that night about the sex, even though she was badly sunburned it did not matter to him just more pain he could inflict. Amy was tough and took what he had to hand out with little or no screaming. This made him mad and determined to get screams out of her the next night.

The next night he used some of the things he learned off the internet to make her scream with pain. He whipped her and cut her and then having sex in every position possible. Amy was no good for work the next day and there was nothing he could do but use Bertha in the gardens.

Amy would get better in a couple of days and fall in with the rest of them each day working the fields and each night when he came for her.

CHAPTER THIRTY TWO

LIFE SETTLES DOWN again for about three years before another incident happens. This means Bertha has now been here fourteen years, longer than any of the other women. She does not know why he has not killed her yet but she thanks God every day.

The last three years could have been much harder than the daily work in the gardens, getting up wood or having sex each night. But the women are now adjusted to this life style and just thankful to be alive.

It seems that all are doing ok until the summer of the third year when they wake one morning to find Carol missing. They look all around the bunkhouse inside and out before calling him to come help find her.

When he comes to the bunkhouse and finds out what's wrong he gets the dogs and shows them Carol's boots. The dogs get the scent and head off looking for her.

Everyone follows the dogs until they get to the lake where they fish and swim. There is Carol's body floating in the lake. He sends the dogs in after her body.

They knew this was suicide because Carol could swim. She must have swum out as far as she could and then tried to late to swim back.

No one had any idea that Carol was thinking about committing suicide and this was really hard to take.

He told them to get back to the bunkhouse and have breakfast and then get to work. Bertha was going to have to cover for Carol until he could find a replacement. He was on his way to the ravine with Carol's body.

CHAPTER THIRTY THREE

A S LUCK WOULD have it, before he could make up his mind where to go and get a woman one drops in his lap.

It was the day after Carol's suicide that a woman came knocking at his door. He looked out the woman and found she was alone.

The woman introduced herself as Linda and she was selling condos in the islands and she wanted to know if he was interested. Seeing she was middle aged and in good shape he said yes and asked her in.

He took her to the kitchen and asked her to have a seat at the kitchen table. He said my cleaning lady has not been in and the rest of the house is a mess. He offered her a drink of coffee, milk or juice that's all he had. She asked for a glass of water, which he got her. He stated that his glass of juice was in the other room and he would be right back. When he came back he had his gun in hand.

He told her to undress or he would kill her right then and there. Linda was in shock and didn't move as fast as he wanted so he slapped her and she screamed but got undressed.

He then told her that this would be her home for the rest of her life and then told her the rest of the rules. He said out the back door and down the steps. Since it was almost suppertime he took her to Bertha in the bunkhouse and told her to tell Linda what happens when the rules are not followed.

This was the easiest woman he had gotten yet; all he had to do was get rid of her car. He knew a perfect place it was an old stone quarry in the mountains about five miles up the road. It was about halfway between his place and a very small town.

He took Linda's car to the quarry and let it roll in and sink to the bottom.

Now all he had to do was walk the mile and half out to the main road and then five miles home. His luck held out again as a trucker stopped and offered him a ride. He told the driver it was only a few miles down the road but the driver said it was ok, that it was to be hot to be walking.

Once in the truck the driver named Paul asked him what he was doing out walking in this heat. He said that he took his car to be worked on in town and they did not have anyone to take him home. He had to be home for an appointment at 8 o'clock. It didn't take much more time to tell the story than they were at his home. The driver dropped him off and went on his way. As the truck passed he checked the license plate and it was from Oklahoma and he knew that the driver would never think about having picked him up again.

He knew someone would come looking for Linda but all he had to say was he had not seen her.

Back at the bunkhouse Linda was answering questions faster than she could ask them. This was the first time that they had meant someone who knew where they were and what was going on in the world outside of there. Linda said she was from a small town down the mountain called Brandonville, West, VA. She was divorced and worked for a realest office there. She had no children because her ex-husband did not want any and this is why they divorced. She said she was 52 years old and worked out a lot to stay in shape.

Her parents Susan and Mark would miss her not calling tonight and not coming home by morning. They would call the police to look for her. At first this gave hope to the women, but they know he was smart enough to get rid of the evidence.

Now they filled Linda in on what happens when the rules are not followed.

Linda began to cry and they told her not to because it was one of the things that turned him on. The other was not to scream anymore that she could help because once turned on he would hurt her more.

He came for supper with them that evening and could not keep his eyes off her.

Later that night he came and took Linda. The crying and screaming was very hard to take since it had been a while since anyone new had been there.

The next morning Linda was hurt to bad to walk so he said she could rest up one day only. Then she went to work helping with the apples and pumpkins. She was lucky that the real hard work was over until late fall and the getting up of the wood would begin.

CHAPTER THIRTY FOUR

THAT FALL AROUND November the women again awoke to find one of them missing.

Barbara had been down in the dumps since Carol had drowned and they knew she might do something stupid.

Barbara and Carol had been very close friends and told each other everything. She knew that Carol had been pregnant and didn't want the monster's baby. But she didn't know that Carol was going to commit suicide.

They sent for him and the dogs again when they could not find her. While he went to get the dogs they put on their ski suits so they could follow.

Again they followed the dogs but not toward the lake. The dogs went down along the fence line until they came to Barbara's body hanging from the fence.

Barbara's body had gotten hung on the barbwire and was hanging down almost within reach. She bled to death and it was really gruesome to see.

He again told them to go back to the bunkhouse while he got her body down and took it to the ravine. The women went back to breakfast and ate in silence.

CHAPTER THIRTY FIVE

NOW IT WAS time to find another woman. He had to think about this a lot. He didn't know whether to use the pick-up in the parking lot or the Laundromat or something new.

He thought about just driving to a big town and working the streets. He would just have to be very careful of being seen.

He thought about picking up a prostitute on a street corner at night if it seemed safe.

He again threw a dart at the map to pick a big city and then to the computer to find the seedy part of town to try in. This time he would be gone a week or maybe longer round trip. He had picked Washington, DC this time. He went out and found tags to use from an old van parked in the woods. He would use these only on the night he would pick-up a woman.

He told his girls he usually would wait till spring to get someone but he wanted this one trained and broke in by spring. He told them he would be gone a week and they better behave or get the whip when he came back. They had all the food they would need.

He left the next day and drove two days to go to downtown DC. Once there he drove the streets at night to see what was going on. He found a lot of hobos and street people around the poorer sections of town. What he was looking for worked the street corners between the not so poor and rich sections of town.

He drove trying to find a woman working by herself and finally late at about 1 o'clock in the morning he found a young white woman standing on a corner with no one around. He stopped and got out and went to talk to her holding his map. When she saw his face she said I can't help you. He pulled out his gun and said I bet you will, now get in the van. She got in the van and before locking it he asked for her purse and what her name was. She said it was Wanda.

He drove out of town and stopped on a back street to change the tag and throw the old one in the dumpster.

Once on the country roads he would stop to sleep and check on Wanda. Wanda needed to pee and he said to get out on go right there on the side of the road. He told her he would get them something to eat in the morning. Wanda asked what he was going to do to her and he said if I can wait that long you will find out in a couple of days.

Wanda never tried anything because she knew what it was liked to be shot. One of her pimps had been very angry when she didn't bring in as much money as he thought she should have and shot her in the shoulder. The pimp would not get a doctor since it was flesh wound. It still hurt like hell. So she wanted nothing to do with guns.

After two days of traveling he was home with her. He told her to get out of the van and get undressed. He told her the rules and said you need a bath lets go to the bunkhouse.

The women could not wait to hear Wanda's story. Wanda had run away from home when she was seventeen and ended up being a prostitute instead of an office manager. She was now twenty years old, 5' 10", slender build and her family would never know what happened to her.

Wanda had grown up in Kansas on a corn farm. She was a high school cheerleader and dating the head of the science class. When her boyfriend dumped her for another girl and she did not know what to do it hurt so bad. Every day she had to see them together and the rest of the kids seemed to laugh at her. Her grades dropped and she just could not get it together so she decided to run a way. She had heard that if you went to the big town of Washington, DC you could get a government job. So she caught a bus and headed to DC.

Once in bus terminal in DC she did not know where to go from there and she was hungry and things didn't look as bright as when she left out.]A man named Big Papa found her and offered her food and a place to stay. But once at the cathouse she found out what it all was going to cost her.

Now she would only have one man after her instead of ten or so a night. She thought this was going to be a blessing compared to what she had at the cathouse. The women told her that she would think differently once he got his hands on her and that the pain would be more than her young body could handle and then some. Wanda said she could handle anything.

That night when he came for her she screamed and cried just like all the rest of them had at the start. Again Bertha had to make him leave Wanda alone because he messed her up so bad. Wanda never had much to say after that night. But she thought a broken heart was way better than all she had been through. Even though the women try to console Wanda she becomes a shadow of herself and does only what he tells her to.

CHAPTER THIRTY SIX

THE FALL WAS over and winter had set in again. The women had hauled wood for the last couple of months and so far it had been a mild winter. But it was supposed to be a white Christmas.

Christmas did not mean much to the women anymore; Bertha had gotten tired of telling the story of her now almost forgotten family. The other women only cried at the thought of not having Christmas with their families anymore. So all the women did was to play games and talk a little among themselves.

Living in hell did not leave a lot to talk about either. Wanda (when she came out of her shell) and Linda would talk about what was happening in the outside world before they came to the bunkhouse. Including the fact that the government was broke and so many people were out of jobs. The crime rate was at an all time high. Somehow people seemed to get by and keep the world turning. But all things considered out there was still a whole lot better than here.

CHAPTER THIRTY SEVEN

IT MUST SEEM as if I am telling the same things over and over again. There is never a lot going on in a camp from hell except work, eat, sleep, sex and death.

It was again about three years later when Amy turns up pregnant. No one knows why it took six years for it to happen but it did. She knows that the baby will be a monster like him and she does not want it. Amy is strong minded and always wants to do things her way. That is why she thought she could get rid of the baby by sticking a long tree branch up inside of her and causing a miscarriage. She was wrong because they found her at the far end of the pot garden, where she was working; she had bled to death before anyone knew what she was doing. He got the four wheeler and takes her body to the ravine but he does not understand why Amy killed herself. His mind does not want to wrap itself around the fact that the women would rather die than have his babies.

The women mourned another loss that night after dinner. This was the reason they did not get to close to each other because you never knew when someone was going to die next.

This now leaves Bertha, Patricia, Linda and Wanda so he will have to get a fifth.

CHAPTER THIRTY EIGHT

HE WAS RUNNING out of ideas and ways to get more women. The older he got the uglier he got and it was hard to get women to look at him let alone get close enough to grab.

He needed someone else soon it was summertime and the busy season. He could not take the time and chance to find someone on the internet. So it was either the parking lot pick-up or back to the bars. They seemed the safest to him.

But as luck would have it on his way back from the grocers he saw a women hitch hiking up the mountain. This was very unusual and he stopped and offered her a ride and he was surprised when she answered yes. He told her she would have to ride in the back because his front seat was missing. She said no problem and he got out and opened the door and once she was inside he pointed his gun at her and asked for her purse and bags. He asked her name and it was Brenda.

Brenda only took the offer because it was getting ready to have a bad thunderstorm and she was afraid of them.

Brenda was a 46 year old white woman 5'6" about 110 lbs who had been beaten by her husband and had had enough. She packed a back pack and started walking. She did not care where she landed believing that anywhere was better than here.

Brenda had been picked up by several nice truck drivers and a few others. Thus she ended up on the highway to a worse hell than she left behind.

Once back at the house he had her get out and undress and then he took her to Bertha in the fields and told Bertha to tell her the rules while she showed Brenda how to do her job.

That night after supper the women all gathered around Brenda and wanted to know what was going on in the real world. Brenda was sunburned, tired and in no mood to talk much. She did tell them she was a 46 year old white woman and she had left a mean husband and had only her parents and three sisters she cared about. She said she would probably feel better in the morning and would tell them more then. What Brenda did not understand was she would be very much under the weather come morning once he was done with her.

It seemed that night that he was not as harsh with Brenda as with other new women. They said maybe he was getting older and could no last as long anymore.

The next morning Brenda is withdrawn because she cannot believe that she has left one hell for another much worse. Her mind won't come to grips with what happened last night. The others try to help her but she is not having any of it. Brenda refuses to work and he comes back with the belt and gives her a good beating. She goes further into shock and he said leave her be for today but she better be ready to work the next day.

The others get together after work and decide to try one more time to bring Brenda out of her funk; she has had all day to get over it.

After supper they each take turns trying to talk some sense into her, but do no good. Knowing that he will beat Brenda again Patricia keeps pushing the issues, not knowing that Brenda got a knife without Bertha knowing and has it hidden under her pillow. Patricia forces Brenda into a cat fight and Brenda pulls out the knife but not being good with such things Patricia takes it away from her and accidently stabs Brenda killing her.

Its not much longer before he comes for his nightly visit only to find his most recent pick up dead. He rants and raves using the belt on each of the girls.

Once he lets off enough steam he tells the girls to have her ready in the morning to go to the raven and they are taking her body there.

CHAPTER THIRTY NINE

HE DECIDES TO wait a while and see if he can get by with just four women.

He waits couple of weeks and finds that he is way behind in the fields. His rotating of the women from the vegetables to the pot fields doesn't seem to be working as planned. He thought letting the women do something different each day would make them work better but it only tired them out more. This made them to tired for his brand of fun at night.

So he decided to drive around the countryside and see if he could pick up another hitchhiker. He had logged about 200 miles of back roads and no luck.

So he went back to the old tried and true method of going to a shopping mall. Only this time he used a strip mall in a small town about 300 miles east of home.

He checked the mall out and found that there was a travel agency there which did a lot of late night business. He watched and noticed the woman running the place left late at night alone. The rest of the stores where long closed by then. Her job was working with the rich who went places she never would. She had a rich lady named Betty who was in late one night and left as she was turning out the lights.

He called to Betty thinking she was the lady running the store. Betty asked what he wanted she was in a hurry. He said he needed directions to such and such an address. Betty said she had never heard of it. He asked if she would look at his map and he moved toward her. Betty took one look at him and turned to run. He told her to stop or he would shot, she listened. He told Betty to come and get in his van. Once in the van he took her purse and cell phone.

Once back at the house he realized how beautiful she really was. This was the prettiest 25 year old white woman he had gotten. But she had a mouth on her and would not shut up. It was going to take a lot of beatings and rapes to get her to be quiet.

He took her to Bertha and told her to tell her the rules if she could get a word in edgewise. Bertha set her down and slapped her a couple of times, she stopped talking for a few minutes. Bertha explained the rules one more time, after so many times she had them memorized. Betty did not want to believe a woman of her status could be in a place like this; this had to be a joke. Bertha assured her that it was no joke or bad dream and to get used to it or go crazy.

By suppertime Betty was ready to talk to the others like they were family. She explained that she was married to an airplane pilot and they were very wealthy. They had no children yet. The women told her that when he got through with them that she would not be able to have kids. He did not want any kids to look as ugly as he is. Betty said how bad could it be, the women just looked at each other and told her she would find out tonight. Betty's way of dealing with stress was to talk and talk she did right up until he came in a couple of hours later.

He slapped her around a couple of times until she stopped talking and started screaming. This turned him on and he went at her more than once.

The next day Betty no longer talked she was so scared she just trembled a lot. She just sat on her bunk and would not eat breakfast. When it came time to work she did as she was told. As time went by Betty settled in but never talked like upon arrival.

He was happy he now had five women: Bertha, Patricia, Linda, Wanda and Betty. His crops where doing well and the women where behaving well. He began to wonder what would go wrong next it had been a couple of months since he got Betty and no mishaps.

It turned out he had a right to worry. Because Patricia who had been the leader of the pack and the strongest one of the group would commit suicide by throwing herself into the ravine. It ate at her mind all the things he did to them and finally it was too much.

They woke up to find her not there and began a search for her ending at the ravine. Here they found her boots the only thing she had to leave behind.

CHAPTER FORTY

TIME ONCE AGAIN to hunt; he has begun to hate this because the more he has to hunt the more chances he takes. He wants a safe way to get women but can think of none except maybe the big cities at night. The Ladies of the night are not missed or looked for just replaced.

He decides enough time has gone by that it would be safe to go try New York City. He knows it will take a week round trip so he stocks the pantry in the bunkhouse for the women and leaves them with orders for that week.

He heads out early one morning and has a long day before pulling into a truck stop to rest up.

He gets to sleep around midnight and around 2:00 something he did not expect happens. There is a loud knocking on the van door and it wakes him with a start. He finds a young black woman standing there she is selling blow jobs for $25.00. At first he thinks no way, then when fully awake he realizes this is the best opportunity he could have.

So he gets out of the van and tells the woman that it would be more comfortable in the back of the van. The woman says ok and that her name is Sally and she is a hooker. He said nice to meet her and opens the door of the van. Inviting her in first so he can help her in. Once she is in he pulls out his gun and tells her if she screams she is dead. Sally is very quiet and gives him her purse when he asks for it.

He finds out by Sally's driver license that she is 18 years old, tall and slender and from New York, what a coincidence.

She is a looker with the black mini skirt and green tub top around very large boobs. He almost wants to take her there and then but holds off. He is only a day away from home and can wait tell then.

He decides to move in case someone comes looking for her. He drives toward home a couple of hours and pulls unto a dirt road to sleep again.

The next morning he lets her out to pee and gives her a drink of water and a stale donut. He tells her it won't be long until they are home her last home.

They arrive late that night and he tells her to get out and strip. Once she is done he takes her to the bunkhouse. There he tells her to pick out a bunk and then he strips and takes her there. She fights like a hellion giving him hit after hit and kick after kick. He finally gets tired of it and hits her so hard it knocks her out. This does not stop him, he continues to take what he wants anyway he wants.

Once he is gone the other women wake her and help her clean up. Sally cries and cries because she has only been a hooker a few months and no one has hurt her.

The women tell Sally what could happen every night if he wants it. Sally says she is afraid and what can she do. Linda says just go with the flow and you won't be hurt as bad because fighting pisses him off. Just go to work during the day and wait to see who he picks at night. Bertha said she could fix most wounds but don't fight him and get a broken bone. Because if you can't work you are useless to him and he will throw you in the deep raven to die a terrible death.

Sally says she has a husband named Samuel and 2 sons, Sam Jr & Stanley. Samuel will never stop looking for her. Bertha said think about it child, there was no one around at 2:00 in the morning to see you get in his van and even if there was it looked like you got in without a fight. He drove a day and a half to get here and you have no way of knowing where here is. So don't have false hopes that someone will ever find you.

You will become a missing person and missing hooker at that.

THE NEXT MORNING Sally is very sore and black and blue, she can't eat he jaw hurts to much. He tells her to take the day off but be ready for work in the morning. Sally thanks him and tells the rest of the women that she is sorry for not doing her part, they all understand they all have been there.

Bertha takes Sally under her wing like a daughter and Sally loves her for it. By the end of the day she can move around a little better and unless he takes her again tonight she should be able to work in the morning. Sally's luck hold he takes Wanda that night.

Sally reports for breakfast and work, not knowing how hard she will be required to work. He has her hoeing in the pot fields and she must hoe half an acre by lunch. Then help get food out of the gardens until suppertime. She hangs in there sunburn, blisters and all.

CHAPTER FORTY TWO

TIME FLIES BY and its wintertime again. The women have to get wood up for the wood stove in the bunkhouse. Linda and Wanda gather the wood that Betty and Sally help cut up. He uses the four wheeler to haul the wood to the shed. They are about to quit for lunch when the unexpected happens. Linda and Wanda are gathering the last of the cut wood when an old tree falls and lands on both of them killing them instantly.

Everyone is in shock and they try to get them out from under the tree but to no avail. He says to cut up the tree just where the bodies are and he will take Linda and Wanda to the ravine.

He mutters the whole time that he will have to go hunting again come spring. He is so tired of having to go out in the real world; he does not count the farmers market that he would almost try to get by with three women again. But he knows deep down that that won't work. So come spring he will think of some new way to get women.

CHAPTER FORTY THREE

A S YOU ALL know from chapter one, he went out and found Sue and me in my front yard. We have come full circle in such a short time it seems there should be more pain and suffering in this book than I have written about. But he does not talk about what he does to the women; it does not turn him on as you would think. He acts almost ashamed of what he did; I get the gory details from the women left and my own experiences.

I know this book is almost finished and I have not come any closer to finding out the locks combination for the back door. There is only one thing I have noticed and that is the hasp is in bad shape and maybe could be forced, we shall see.

CHAPTER FORTY FOUR

ONE DAY WHEN he heads off to market he leaves us with our chores to do that day while he is gone along with the tools we will need. Once he is gone for the whole day we start work. About eleven o'clock I stop and take by hoe and go up on the back porch. I put the hoe handle between the hasp and the wall and pull. The hasp screws begin to come loose, but I need help. I call Sue to come help pull on the hoe handle. Sue is scared he will return and find us, but she comes to help. We pull and pull and finally the hasp gives and we are home free. I call Betty, Sally and Bertha to come with us to get free and all come running.

CHAPTER FORTY FIVE

ONCE IN THE house we search the place over for anything we can use. I find the phone and call the police. I tell them who we are and that they will have to trace the call because we do not know where we are. They say they are on their way to stay put.

We search the house and find the basement where there is a pile of cloths, a pile of purses and a pile of shoes. We sort thru and find something that fits, our own cloths are now way too big for us.

There is an old dresser full of cell phones no long any good, he has removed the batteries and thrown them away.

CHAPTER FORTY SIX

ONCE THE POLICE arrive they set up a trap for him, but when he arrives he pulls a gun and puts up a fight which he loses. The police shoot and kill him.

Bertha can't stand him being dead and runs into the road and gets killed by a tractor trailer.

I ask the police if they would tell Bertha's family that he beat her to death and then he was killed. For it seems Bertha fell in love with the monster back in the beginning and she was his spy that's why he treated her so well. But her family does not need to know all that, after all this time has passed. The police agree and they will tell her family a special ending.

The tractor trailer driver was sent on his way with no charges.

The four of us are put in a helicopter and sent to the nearest hospital down the Tennessee Mountains we were on. Our families are contacted and told to meet us there.

The worst is over but the nightmares will go on forever.

THE END